My friends are coming over
for a valentine treat.

We'll have a lot of goodies
and, of course, they'll all be sweet.

I'll make a valentine,
or maybe I'll make two.

They're for someone special.
Can you guess who?

Baking heart-shaped cookies is so much fun.

I wish I could eat them all— every single one!

My valentine teddy
is as cute as he can be.

He's soft and warm and cuddly,
and he sleeps with me.

"Flowers for Mommy."
That's what Daddy said.

The colors are so pretty —
pink and white and red.

"Be my valentine!"
is what people say
whenever they meet
on this holiday.

Happy Valentine's Day!